ERIC STERLING
SECRET AGENT

Trouble at Bamboo Bay

ERNEST HERNDON

ZondervanPublishingHouse
Grand Rapids, Michigan

A Division of HarperCollinsPublishers

Other books in the Eric Sterling series

The Secret of Lizard Island
Double-Crossed in Gator Country
Night of the Jungle Cat
Smugglers on Grizzly Mountain
Sisters of the Wolf

For Matthew Cody

Trouble at Bamboo Bay
Copyright © 1996 by Ernest Herndon

Requests for information should be addressed to:

📖 ZondervanPublishingHouse
Grand Rapids, Michigan 49530

Library of Congress Cataloging-in-Publication Data

Herndon, Ernest.
    Trouble at Bamboo Bay / Ernest Herndon.
        p.   cm.—(Eric Sterling, secret agent : 6)
    Summary: While hiking in Hawaii, twelve-year-old Eric discovers a val-
ley where a young girl lives the ancient ways of her ancestors, and a criminal tries to set up a drug smuggling operation.
    ISBN: 0–310–20730–4 (softcover)
    [1. Adventure and adventurers—Fiction.   2. Christian life—Fiction.
3. Hawaii—Fiction.]   I. Title.   II. Series: Herndon, Ernest. Eric Sterling,
secret agent : #6.
PZ7.H43185Tr 1996
[Fic]—dc 20   96–24624
                                                                            CIP
                                                                             AC

Illustrations by Gloria Oostema

Printed in the United States of America

97 98 99 00 01 02 03 /❖ DH/ 10 9 8 7 6 5 4 3 2

1

As soon as I got the big news I went straight to my friends' house. Ax was in his room pumping iron and his sister Sharon was in their dad's veterinary clinic behind the house treating a fungus on a king snake. At my request they dropped what they were doing and joined me on their patio.

"So what's the news?" Sharon asked.

"First, I need a tape player," I said, holding up a cassette.

"Why don't you just tell us what's up?" Ax said. "You don't have to be so mysterious."

"He wants to make us figure it out, like detectives," Sharon guessed with a grin.

"Considering how many cases we've handled as secret agents, you ought to be able to figure out something as simple as this," I said.

Ax shrugged his muscular shoulders and went into the house, returning with a battery-powered cassette player. He slipped in my tape and turned it on.

"Hey, the Beach Boys," Sharon said when the music started. "'Surfin' Safari.'"

Ax frowned at his sister. "You like that stuff?"

"A lot of kids do," she retorted.

"Pay attention," I said. I pretended to stand on a surfboard and held my arms out, waving them up and down as though trying to keep my balance on a big wave.

"So this is like charades, huh?" Ax said. "OK—I know! You're playing a giant gooney bird in the school play!"

"Ha ha."

"No, Ax," Sharon said. "The song is 'Surfin' Safari.' That's a clue. Safari, get it? Eric is going to Africa. See? He's riding a runaway elephant."

I cut the tape off. "Very funny, you guys. Some detectives you are."

"So tell us what it is," Ax said, wandering over to a heavy bag hanging from a tree limb, and tapping it with some punches.

"Yeah, I've got to get back to my snake," Sharon said, glancing at the concrete block building where her dad kept sick animals from the zoo where he worked.

"I'm going to Hawaii, on vacation!" I announced proudly.

"Hawaii! Cool!" Ax said, giving his bag a karate kick with the speed only a black belt could muster.

"Just you?" Sharon teased. "What about us?"

"Yeah, let's get Miss Spice to give us an assignment *there*," Ax said.

Miss Spice was our boss at Wildlife Special Investigations, the CIA branch where we worked. Even though Sharon and I were only twelve and Ax thirteen, WSI had picked us to be secret agents. Actually, it was *because* of our ages that they chose us, since crooks wouldn't be likely to suspect kids of being spies.

"I already asked her," I said. "She didn't have any work that needs doing there right now. She just told me to go and enjoy myself for a week."

"That figures," Ax complained. "She's always sending us to swamps and jungles, but when we get a chance to go to Hawaii, sorry, no dice."

"Oh, Ax, you know it's fun wherever she sends us," Sharon said.

"Fun?" I interjected. "Dangerous is more like it."

"So what are you going to do in Hawaii, I mean besides surf?" Ax asked me.

"My dad has an old friend who lives there, on the big island," I said. "We'll be staying with him."

"The big island?" Ax said.

"Don't you remember from social studies?" Sharon said. "You ought to. You always make straight A's."

"Oh yeah," Ax said, continuing to punch and kick the bag lightly. He wore gym shorts and a muscle shirt, and sweat glistened on his tan skin in the summer's heat. "I remember now. There's a bunch of islands."

"Let me see if we've got a map," Sharon said. She went inside and was back out in a few minutes with a big blue foldout.

"Neat! Where'd you get that?" I asked as she spread it out on a table.

"It came in one of Dad's magazines. He saves all the maps and puts them on a shelf in the back room."

Ax stood beside us and began reading names of the islands. "Maui, Oahu—"

"That's where Honolulu is," Sharon said.

"—Kauai, Molokai, Lanai, Hawaii, plus these little ones. How many are you going to see?"

"Just the big one, the one named Hawaii. I mean, we'll have a stopover at Honolulu. But Dad said we'd save money if we just stay on the big island where his friend lives."

"Too bad you can't see the others while you're there," Sharon said.

"You know parents." I sighed. "Always trying to save money."

"You'll be gone a week?" Ax asked.

"That's right. And I want to learn how to surf. That would be cool."

"From what I hear, it's not as easy as it looks," Ax warned. "Surfers get killed sometimes in those big waves."

"Killed!" I said.

"That's if the sharks don't get them first."

Sharon threw a twig at her brother. "Oh, leave him alone, Ax. You're just jealous."

She reached over and turned the tape player back on. "Come on, Eric, let's go surfing."

We jumped on imaginary surfboards and caught a wave.

2

It felt strange to be on a plane with my parents instead of Ax and Sharon. Usually we kids were headed off to some dangerous adventure in a far-off place. Not this time, though. Nope, this trip would be pure pleasure.

My parents let me have the window seat, which was great for a while. When the pilot gave the OK to use electronic devices, I listened to the Beach Boys on my Walkman, to get into the mood. But by the third "Surfin' Safari" I'd had about all I could stand.

Mom sat next to me working crossword puzzles. Dad, in the aisle seat, was asleep with his mouth open.

I didn't mind traveling with my parents. In some ways it was kind of neat. But there was one thing that bothered me.

Green shoes.

My dad insisted on wearing these green canvas sneakers. Now I don't expect my father to be fashionable. No hope for that. But wearing green shoes wasn't just nerdy, it was weird. He had them on now, one foot stuck out in the aisle, and I could only hope no one would think I was traveling with him.

I was asleep when we landed at Honolulu late at night. My parents said later they walked me down the corridors like a pet zombie to the island-hopper plane that would take us to the big island. I don't really remember much about it.

I woke up when we landed at Hilo, though. The small airport, open on the sides, was full of tropical night smells. Dad's friend, Jay Johnson, was there to meet us with his sixteen-year-old son Todd.

Jay was my dad's friend from high school, and as soon as they saw each other they did some goofy handshake. Then Jay shook our hands normally and introduced us to Todd.

Todd was cool. He wore cutoff jean shorts, a muscle shirt and flip-flops. He was small for his age, muscular but lean, and very tan. His thick brown hair was streaked from the sun. He grinned when we met and gave me the thumbs-up—only I noticed he stuck his pinkie out too.

"That's *shaka*," he explained when I asked him about it as we walked to the parking lot. "It means, like, hey, how you doing?"

I tried it. It felt cool.

They had a pickup truck, and Todd and I rode in the back with the luggage.

"We're lucky it's not raining," Todd told me as we whisked through the warm Hawaiian night.

"How long have you lived here?" I asked.

"Two years. We moved here from California."

"Do you surf?" I asked him.

"Some. I like hiking better."

"Hiking? In Hawaii?"

"Sure. We've got all kinds of great trails here on the big island. I'll show you my guidebook when we get home. Ever do any backpacking?"

"Oh yeah."

"Maybe we can do some while you're here."

My pulse shot up. The fun was already starting. "But I didn't bring any gear," I said.

"We've got plenty."

Todd lived pretty far out of town. His house stood at the end of a long gravel driveway. Todd's mom, Martha, was waiting for us with a pitcher of passion fruit drink.

Their house was big and rambling, with shiny wooden floors. I put my suitcase in Todd's room. Even though it was close to midnight—we had crossed a few time zones—he pulled a book down from his shelf.

"Look at these hiking trails," he said. "Mauna Kea, Waimanu Valley, Kau Desert—"

"Did you say desert?"

"The big island's got everything, dude. Even snowcapped mountains."

"Wow!" A map showed the island was laced with trails. "Have you done all of these?" I asked.

"A bunch. There's a new one I want to do that's not in here. Bamboo Bay Natural Area. They just opened it. Real remote. They say it's like stepping back in time."

"Sounds cool."

"Did you bring any boots at all?"

"Just tennis shoes."

He stroked his chin, which had downy blond hairs. "That'll do. We could hike it tomorrow, camp a couple nights, maybe even three."

"Great!" My worst nightmare was being stuck at the house while Dad and his friend talked about old times for days on end. Still, I had my heart set on catching a wave. "Will we get to do any surfing?"

"We can. The big island's not great for surfing, not like Oahu. Boogie boards are fun. We could do that when we get back."

"What's a boogie board?"

He laughed. "You are a *haole*, aren't you?" He pronounced it "howlie."

13

"Now I'm really lost."

"*Haole* means outsider. It's what Hawaiians call people from the mainland, especially tourists. A boogie board's like a surfboard but shorter. You lie on top of it. So, you up for a hiking trip?"

"You bet!"

"I'll go ask my folks."

I followed him nervously. Our parents agreed readily, probably glad to get their kids out of their hair for the next few days so they could visit. We would leave in the morning.

When I finally turned in I was so excited I could hardly sleep.

3

I woke to the smell of coffee. But the air was so chilly I hated to get out of bed. We had slept with the window open, and I never would have thought Hawaii could be so nippy!

For breakfast we ate muffins, strawberry papayas and apple bananas, which were short, plump bananas with an apple-like flavor.

When we finished eating we went to the storeroom and hauled out the camping gear we needed. It took a while to pack, but we finally carried two heavy backpacks outside.

The Johnsons had two pickups, and we put our stuff in the old one. It was faded turquoise with a rusted tailgate. The motor made a deep rumble and spewed blue smoke out the tailpipe. Springs stuck up in the front seat. I liked it.

Rain drizzled as we drove through Hilo, past a beach and palm trees, out along the coast. The gray sea lay to our right, jungly hills to our left. Todd turned the radio to a country station. That's what all his friends listened to, he said. He pulled a round can of smokeless tobacco from the glove compartment, stuck a pinch in his lip, and offered me some.

It smelled minty. I took a dab and wedged it against my lower gum, where it burned the tender skin. Then I propped my elbow in the open window like Todd did and nodded to the twang of a steel guitar—the kind of music I don't normally listen to since my dad likes it.

The rain stopped and the sun came out, turning the ocean a sparkling blue. From the highway you could see across it for miles. Todd put on a pair of black sunglasses; I wished I had some.

We passed huge sugarcane fields, and strands of rain forest where I caught sweet whiffs of tropical flowers. I was really enjoying the ride, until I started feeling dizzy. It came on slow at first, then got bad fast. I turned my face toward the window, slipped the tobacco out of my mouth, and tossed it out. Whew! I needed a drink, but the canteens were in the back.

"Are we going to stop anytime soon?" I asked casually, spitting flecks of snuff out.

"There's a town right up here. Want a cold drink?"

"Yeah!"

When we entered the town, Todd pulled to the curb, radio blaring. I climbed out and staggered into a nearby fruit market where I bought a bottle of cold mango juice. Thank goodness! It washed away the funky taste and made me feel a little better.

When I came out, Todd was standing on the sidewalk talking to a couple of girls. The one who seemed to be his age had long blond hair and a golden tan. She appeared real interested in the conversation, but the other girl, who looked my age, seemed bored. She was cute too, with short brown hair.

"This is Eric," Todd said when I walked up. "We're headed for Bamboo Bay. Backpacking."

"Cool," the blond girl said, pronouncing it "coouhl."

I glanced at the other girl a couple times, but she never looked at me. I was probably just a dumb *haole* to her. I didn't have much of a tan, and my blue-green jams were so baggy they made my legs resemble sticks. Still too woozy to care, I went to the truck and waited in the front seat. I finished my juice and closed my eyes.

After a while Todd got in and cranked the engine, gunning it. It sounded like a race car. He pulled out with screeching tires, flipping the girls a *shaka*. In the rearview mirror, I saw the older girl return the gesture.

"I'm telling you, Eric, Hawaii is babe city," Todd said. "That young one was pretty cute too, huh? I saw you checking her out."

I shook my head. How little he knew me. "Todd, I'm into action—not girls."

"Is that so?" He chuckled.

We arrived at the Bamboo Bay Natural Area parking lot in midmorning. There was only one other vehicle in it.

"Not many people hike here, huh?" I said.

Todd shrugged. "It's new. Hasn't caught on yet. I like the trails better before they get discovered."

We got out, and that's when I noticed how high the mountain was. It was a sheer green wall with a trail zigzagging up it.

"Uh, do we go over that?" I asked.

"I thought you were a backpacker, dude."

"Yeah, not a mountain climber. That looks like Mount Everest!"

"You can handle it."

We checked out the park sign, which had a map on it. It showed a crooked trail wiggling over the mountain to a valley.

"See how small the valley is?" Todd said, pointing to the map. "It was owned by some rich ranchers who never did anything to it. But the state wanted it for a natural area and bought it. I heard there were some old-time Hawaiians living back in there, too."

"What happened to them?" I asked.

"Evicted, I guess. It's public property now."

We signed our names in the register at the trail-head, then returned to the truck and got our gear in order. Todd wore ragged jean cutoffs, a muscle shirt, and thick socks under heavy-duty hiking boots. I had on my baggy jams and a grizzly bear T-shirt, tennis shoes, and a cap. We hefted the heavy packs and Todd led the way onto the trail.

Soon we were climbing. The path led through short brush with occasional stands of trees. I could see the ocean off to the right and the parking lot down below.

Todd was in good shape and got way ahead of me. He had to wait while I came up huffing, puffing, and sweating.

"Doing all right?" he asked. I was afraid he would tease me but he didn't.

"I'd be doing better if I hadn't tried that tobacco," I admitted.

He nodded. "Yeah, seems like it cuts your wind. I've been meaning to give it up."

"It made me dizzy."

"You'll make it, dude. Just hang in there."

It took over an hour to reach the top, and I was hurting. The trail entered forest, and Todd stopped to rest in a grove of trees. Some of them were Australian pines, he said, and their needles carpeted the ground. We took off our packs and sat down against tree trunks. I removed my cap so the wind would dry my sweaty hair.

"Feel that breeze?" Todd said. "Ocean's not far."

"Feels great."

"Hey, look." He jumped up. "Mountain apples."

He picked some small pink fruits and tossed one to me.

"Is this really an apple?" I asked, watching him bite down.

He nodded. "Hawaiian. Try it."

I bit. It was crisp and juicy. It made me think of autumn, something they never had here in the tropics. Too bad.

We ate a few, then resumed hiking. The trail stayed pretty level, dipping now and then to cross a creek. The apples, the rest, and the easier trail made me feel better. So did the breeze and the sweet smells.

After a few hours, the trail turned and began to go down. A sharp bend gave us a view of the valley and the sea. "Bamboo Bay," Todd said.

"Wow." Dark blue water glistened between two mountain shoulders. Rain forest cloaked the narrow valley. "Like the Garden of Eden."

Just then we heard a gunshot below.

Todd frowned. "There's not supposed to be any hunting in the park." He looked at me. "Sounds like there's trouble in Eden."

4

"Maybe somebody just brought a gun for target practice," I said.

He nodded. "Probably."

We hiked on, hearing more shots now and then, and were halfway down the mountainside when a man and a woman came walking quickly up the trail. They were breathing hard, their faces red. They were dressed like regular backpackers— shirts, shorts, boots, packs—except for stiff brown leggings from their ankles to their knees, probably to keep from scratching their legs. The man, who had a brown beard, shook his head when he saw us.

"Better go back," he said, barely stopping. "There's a crazy person down there with a gun."

"What's the deal?" Todd said.

"I don't know, but we're getting out. I'd advise you to do the same."

Just then a bullet whizzed through the trees overhead. We ducked. A leaf drifted down.

"You going to call the police?" Todd asked as the hikers hurried on.

The man stopped suddenly. "Uh, don't worry about the police. We'll take care of it."

Another bullet whistled by.

"Come on, George," the woman said in a panicky voice. The hikers vanished up the trail.

"Let's vamoose," Todd said.

But I had an idea. "Wait."

He looked at me questioningly.

"I'm going down to check it out," I said.

"Are you crazy?"

I hesitated, trying to decide how much to tell him. "Todd, I know this will sound strange, but I'm a federal agent. This is strictly confidential, but I think you need to know. I work for Wildlife Special Investigations, a branch of the CIA. And I think I should go see what's the matter."

Todd stared at me, then burst into laughter. I think it was the jams. "Eric, this is no time for jokes." He doubled over and held his stomach from laughing so hard.

"I'm serious, Todd. For real."

Todd was having trouble breathing. "I've heard about keeping your sense of humor when things get tough, but this beats everything."

"I'm not joking."

He straightened up, examined me, laughed some more, then frowned suddenly. "You *are* serious, aren't you?"

"If I had my badge with me I'd show you, but I'm on vacation."

"Well I'll be, dude. I never would have had you pegged for a—for a—" He burst into laughter again. "A secret—" He collapsed and lay on his back, his feet sticking up like a bug.

A bullet pinged on a rock nearby. Todd got solemn in a hurry, scrambling to his feet. "Come on, let's go, Eric."

"I'm going down, Todd. I mean it."

"Look, even if you are some kind of secret agent or something, I can't let you go down there. Your parents would kill me."

"My parents know I'm an agent. They'll understand." Actually, they'd probably throw a fit. "Tell you what," I added. "Wait for me in the parking lot. It shouldn't take long." I tried to sound official.

Todd shook his head. "This is ridiculous."

Another bullet zipped by.

"Look, I'm out of here," Todd said. "Those other hikers said they'd call the police, but that'll take a while. Sorry, dude, but I'm going back to the truck. Just be careful!"

He hurried up the trail, crouching slightly, his boots clattering noisily. From far up the mountainside I could hear the worried voices of the other two fleeing hikers.

It suddenly dawned on me what I was doing. Was I crazy? I wanted to impress people, that's all. Like that girl back in town. If I broke this case I could wind up in the papers. I bet she'd pay attention then!

Keeping low, I picked my way down the trail. There were no more gunshots, but that just made me more nervous, never knowing when the next bullet would fly. I tried to walk quickly but silently, which wasn't easy on the slick, rocky trail. At least the forest concealed me.

As I picked my way down the trail I tried to come up with a plan of action. Taking out snipers was not exactly my specialty. If only Ax and Sharon were here to help me come up with a strategy. After all, I could get shot!

It occurred to me that this case had nothing to do with wildlife. I was out of my jurisdiction. If the gunman were shooting at animals, that would be different. But he was firing at people. That made it the business of a SWAT team, not a WSI agent.

A noise below startled me. I crouched behind a tree and peered down the slope through the jungle.

A wild hog trotted quickly along, maybe frightened by the gunfire, too. Perhaps it *was* my jurisdiction. I continued down the trail.

I had almost reached the valley floor when I caught sight of a sunny patch on a boulder. And there, sitting on a rock, was the gunman! He must have figured everyone was gone, and now he appeared to be rubbing his rifle down.

I couldn't make out many details through the trees. His back was to me, and he was wearing a black shirt.

Quietly I slipped off my backpack. Then I picked up a sturdy stick, and crept through the woods.

Conditions were perfect. The wind rattling the branches disguised any sounds I might have made. The wavering shadows would have made me hard to see even if the gunman hadn't had his back turned.

When I reached the edge of the small clearing I had a better view, but it was still hard to make out details in the dazzling sunlight. I knew if I stopped to think I'd get scared. I needed to act now!

Gripping the stick tightly, I sprang out of the forest, dashed across the boulder, and kicked the rifle away. The gunman whipped around to face me— and I got the shock of my life.

The "gunman" was a girl, hardly older than I!

5

Stopping to stare was a big mistake. She slammed a kick against the side of my knee, causing me to buckle. Then she grabbed my head in both hands and drove her knee into my forehead.

Eeyow! I saw the Milky Way.

I shook it off when I saw her going for the gun. I made a diving tackle and sent her sprawling on her face. She writhed around and hammered my head with her fists, but I held on, working my way up till I could grab her arms. I pinned her flat against the rock on her back. We were both breathing hard.

The girl stared at me with savage anger. I had her trapped and she knew it. My main concern now was the gun. Holding her down with my knees, I reached over and grabbed it. Quickly I removed the clip and ejected the bullet from the chamber. My WSI training told me it was a twenty-two caliber bolt-action with no scope. I slid the clip and bullet into the pocket of my jams and was leaning over to lay the rifle down when she bucked.

I did a somersault and landed on my back, dazed. The girl jumped up and dashed into the bushes. As I got to my feet I saw a white horse, mostly screened by leaves, tethered to a tree. The girl untied the horse, leaped on its back with the skill of a cowboy, wheeled around, and galloped away.

Bruised and aching, all I could do was watch her go.

At least I had the gun. And this was a small valley. She couldn't get far.

Carrying the rifle, I staggered back to the trail and reloaded the rifle just in case she had more weapons. Then I hefted the pack and set off down the path.

The trail led onto the valley floor where trees stood bigger than ever. Virgin rain forest, I figured. A clear stream slid through the trees, and I stepped from stone to stone to cross it. The trail ended at a shoreline of smooth, rounded rocks, some as big as coffee tables. The blue sea surged against them noisily, knocking them against each other.

The girl was nowhere in sight. She must be back up the valley.

I returned to the stream and followed it up through the jungle. When I spotted some fresh horse droppings I knew I was on the right track.

Before long, a narrow path left the creek. As I walked quietly along, I heard a sound like someone crying. At a clearing I saw a small, grassy cemetery. The girl knelt in front of a grave while the horse grazed nearby.

The girl held her stomach and rocked back and forth as if in pain, sobbing uncontrollably. I felt sorry for her all of a sudden. I didn't know what her story was, but it had to be bad.

I walked up behind her, clearing my throat so I wouldn't startle her. She didn't even look around.

I knelt beside her. What I had earlier mistaken for a black shirt was in fact her long dark hair hanging down her back. She wore incredibly baggy shorts and shirt, like a man's hand-me-down clothes. She was barefoot, and the soles of her feet looked tough. Her brown skin made me figure she was a true Hawaiian.

The little graveyard held four graves, each with a wooden cross.

"Uh, is there something I can, like, do to help?" I asked.

She shook her head. "It hurts so much," she said through her tears.

"Your stomach?"

"No!" she said bitterly. "My grandfather." She nodded at the grave.

Then, as if she could bear to be around me no longer, she rose, hurried to her horse, and climbed on. She urged it into a trot and disappeared down a path into a grove of trees.

With a sigh of confusion, I got to my feet and went after her.

The trail through the grove came out to one of the most beautiful scenes I had ever gazed upon. I was standing near the head of the valley, where it narrowed to a point beneath sheer mountain walls. To the left a waterfall tumbled into a large, rock-rimmed pool, obviously the beginning of the stream I had followed. To the right stood a thatched bamboo house on stilts beneath tall, spreading trees. In the middle lay a lush, green garden, soft in the evening light.

The horse nickered, grazing under the trees. The girl emerged from beneath the house, carrying a hoe over her shoulder. Ignoring me, she headed straight for the garden.

I'd had about enough of this craziness. I ran up and grabbed her arm.

"I don't get it!" I said. "First you try to kill people. Then you want to beat me up. Now you're calmly going to work in your garden. Are you nuts or something?"

She looked at me with glittering eyes. "If I'd wanted to kill those people, they would be dead. This is my valley, not theirs."

"It's a public park!"

She snatched her arm away. "I was born and raised here. My parents and my grandparents lived here. Those people did not belong here, and you don't belong here either. Why don't you go back where you came from, *haole*?"

For a second I thought of my home, my parents. I glanced around. "So where are your parents, anyway?" I asked.

"They're dead! They're all dead. Are you happy now? My mother, my father, my grandmother, and now Grandfather."

"You mean you live here alone?"

Her dark eyes staring at me seemed full of hatred. Then they began to well with tears. I didn't know *what* to do. Comfort her? Walk away?

Suddenly the white horse neighed loudly. We watched it rear up on its hind legs, paw the air, then stumble backward and fall onto its side.

"Cloud!" the girl screamed.

I raced over, but stopped short when I saw a six-foot-long cobra, its flared hood raised beside the horse. The girl came up behind me. I slammed the clip into the gun, chambered a round, took careful aim, and blew the snake's head off. We both stood back as it writhed and died. When it was safe to move, the girl ran to the horse, which lay on its side breathing rapidly.

"She's been bitten!" she said.

I saw bloody fang marks above the right rear knee.

"This can't be!" the girl said, almost hysterical. "There are no snakes in Hawaii!"

I eyed the dead cobra and the ailing horse. "There are now."

6

"Do you know some kind of herbal remedy for snakebite?" I asked the girl.

"I told you, we have no snakes! How would I know a cure?"

I tried to recall everything I'd read about snakebite. First, get to a doctor. Forget that. Second, use a snakebite kit. As if I had one.

In the old days people would try to suck out the poison. But would that even work on a cobra bite? I seemed to remember reading that their fangs and venom were different than, say, a rattlesnake's. Well, I could only try.

I knelt beside the horse and put my mouth to the jagged marks on its rear leg. Then I began to suck.

The taste was bitter and salty. Each time I got some of the blood out I spat it on the ground, then kept sucking. The horse lay still, as if realizing I wanted to help. Time after time I sucked out a tiny amount and spat it out.

At last no more would come. I sat back. And then everything hit me—the tobacco, the long drive, the fight with the girl, the poison. It all came together to make me sick. I raced over to a tree and threw up. Then I sat down, dizzy and weak.

The girl put a cup of water to my lips. I rinsed my mouth and drank. Then she took my arm and led me up the steps into the dark bamboo house. The floor was made of springy cane. There were no windows, but I could tell that two rooms opened onto a large sitting room. She led me through the door on the left and I stretched out on a plank bed covered with a lumpy mattress. "You'd better stay here for the night," she said.

I immediately fell into confused dreams. I saw beautiful green forest, a babbling stream, a pretty girl. But the peaceful images were disturbed by the vision of a wicked snake laughing at me from its hiding place in the bushes.

Once I sat up in the night sweating, not knowing where I was. My heart raced. I nearly panicked. Then the girl came and lowered me gently back down, wiping my forehead with a damp cloth, and I slept.

Sometime before dawn my fever left and I felt cool and relaxed. I slept deeply then, like a thirsty person drinking cold, clear water.

My eyes opened to dim morning light. I sat up, woozy and weak, then staggered to the front door of the hut and gazed out on the valley. Green mountain walls towered into the mist. The waterfall whispered gently. The garden twinkled with dew, and delicious plant smells filled the air.

The horse was nowhere in sight. Neither was the girl.

Then I saw her coming out of the forest carrying a basket. When she saw me she quickened her step.

"I have breakfast," she said, holding up a basket of fruit.

She came up the steps and we sat down on the cane floor, since there was no furniture. She emptied the basket of fruit gently onto a mat.

"Guavas, mangoes, bananas, papayas," she said, sitting back proudly. "Eat."

"Thank you," I said weakly, reaching for a guava. The taste was so sweet it made my heart sing. I hadn't realized how famished I was.

The girl took a butcher knife from her belt and expertly peeled a papaya. She cut it in half and I bit into the juicy orange fruit.

Thank you, Lord.

I ate some of everything. The guavas were my favorite. The bananas were a close second.

"What's your name?" I asked the girl.

"Wailana."

"Waila—" My tongue got tangled.

She smiled. "Wai-la-na. It means peaceful water. You can just call me Lana if it's easier."

"Lah-na. Lana. Yeah, I can do that."

"And your name?"

"Eric. Eric Sterling."

She had trouble pronouncing my name too. I realized English might not be her first language. After a little practice she could say Eric as easily as I could say Lana.

"How is Cloud?" I asked.

The girl's pretty face brightened. "She is OK. In the night she stood up and hobbled to the stream to drink. Then she went into her stall, behind the house. She is there now, resting." Lana put her hand on my arm. "You saved her. Thank you."

I shrugged. "I don't know if what I did really did any good."

She shook her head. "You took her poison. You almost died yourself." She stood abruptly. "Did you get enough food?"

"Yes, thanks."

At the door she gazed toward the waterfall, about a hundred yards away. "Perhaps you would like to wash?"

I realized how grimy I was, and chuckled. "You bet."

"You wash. I must work in the garden."

She had brought my pack into the house. I dug out a pair of purple jams and a T-shirt and went outside. The sun was burning off the mist and the cool morning was turning hot. Flies buzzed around the seeds Lana had thrown on the ground.

Lana got her hoe from under the house. "I threw the snake into the bushes," she said, following me.

I didn't really want to think about the snake right now. Just the thought made me queasy. "What do you grow in your garden?" I asked.

"Do you not see? Taro. Sugarcane. Pineapples. Sweet potatoes."

"What are those big leaves that look like arrowheads?"

Lana stared at me. "That is taro. I thought everyone knew what taro looks like."

"Isn't that a root crop of some kind?"

She laughed, as if deciding I must be joking, and went on to her garden, shaking her head.

I followed the path to the pool. Laying my shoes and clean clothes on a rock, I waded out. Icy! Rocks made walking difficult. When it was deep enough I swam out and, curious, I dove to the bottom. The pool was no more than six feet deep. I swam over to a spot by the falls, which pounded loudly. The water gushed down too hard for me to stand under, but I stood in the cold spray and it felt like a shower.

When I felt clean I swam back across and stepped behind a tree to change. After the breakfast and the cold bath, dressed in clean clothes, I felt like new.

But as I walked back toward the garden, worries flooded me. Where was Todd? Where were the police those hikers promised to call? Would Lana get in trouble for firing the gun? What should I do now?

7

When I reached the garden and Lana smiled, those questions faded. I felt I had entered a place where time did not exist. I wasn't mad at her anymore. Our fight yesterday, and her craziness with the gun, seemed like a silly dream. I knew I should take action—I wanted, now, to protect Lana's home, go to the police and tell them there was no gunman. And I knew I should make sure my parents weren't worrying about me. Later, I told myself. I'll go later.

"Feel better?" she asked.

"Much."

She pulled the butcher knife from her belt and cut a stalk of sugarcane. With skillful movements she removed a joint and sliced away the peel, then cut it into chunks. She tossed me one and crammed one into her mouth. The moist, cool cane was incredibly sweet and juicy. When I had swallowed all the juice I spat the pith out, like she did.

"You raise this garden all by yourself?" I asked.

"My grandfather started it," she said, handing me more cane. "We have always had the taro. When I was little my grandmother went over the mountain and came back with pineapple, sugarcane, and sweet potato. She said taro alone was not enough for a growing girl. Grandfather argued but she won." She smiled at the memory. Then her face clouded. "Grandmother died when I was eight. She wanted me to learn all about the world outside"—she swept her arm toward the mountains—"but Grandfather said that world is no good, and everything I need to know can be found right here in this valley."

"You mean you've never been out of the valley?"

"Never."

I stared at her in awe. "Not even to school?"

"Grandmother taught me to read and write. Grandfather said that's no good, and when she died I had no more lessons."

"What about church?"

"Grandmother read to me from the Bible, but Grandfather also did not like that. When she died he hid the Bible and told me I must worship Pele." She pronounced it Peh-lee.

"Pele?"

Lana again stared at me as if she couldn't believe my ignorance. "The goddess of fire. She rules the island."

Oh yeah, I remembered reading something about that. Ancient Hawaiians thought volcanic eruptions were due to Pele's wrath.

"You mean you don't believe in God or Jesus?"

"Grandmother did, but I don't know." She shrugged and resumed hoeing.

I couldn't believe what I was hearing. Here was a girl who had never been out of this tiny valley, who had never been to school or church. Her very clothes, obviously, were her grandfather's hand-me-downs. And she believed in some kind of goddess!

"So for food, then, you just eat from the garden, and fruit and stuff?"

"Sure." She brushed a long strand of black hair from her face. "The forest is full of fruit trees. There is plenty of breadfruit." She pointed to the trees by the house. "I get fish from the stream and sometimes from the sea. And when I can, I shoot hogs."

"Really? You shoot hogs?"

She scowled. "I hate them. Grandfather told me they don't belong here. They raid the garden. Grandfather would sit up at night with the gun and wait for them. But they are hard to hunt. They are very wise."

The girl amazed me. She was smaller than I, yet strong enough to tend a garden all by herself—a big garden at that—and to fish and even hunt wild hogs! Plus, she was bold enough to try to run intruders out of her valley with a gun!

"Why were you shooting at those hikers yesterday?" I asked, wanting more details.

"Like I said, this is my valley." Her face tightened with anger, but then she relaxed, perhaps remembering I was not her enemy. "We have lived here forever. Then the officers came and told Grandfather we must move."

"Officers?"

She nodded. "They said the valley is a public park, that we have no right to live here. Grandfather told them that the ranchers own the land and have always let us stay here. But they said the ranchers sold them the land and we must leave. That is when Grandfather took sick." Her voice trailed off.

"And then he died," I said softly.

She hung her head sadly.

"Don't you have any family outside the valley?"

She glanced up with a flash of anger. "What does it matter? This is my valley. I am not leaving."

I held up my hands. "OK, OK. I'm not telling you to leave." But I knew it was hopeless. The officials would never let her stay. Sooner or later they would force her out—if they didn't shoot her in a gun battle first.

"Can I see Cloud?" I said, changing the subject.

The girl smiled. Her moods were as changeable as the breezes that swept across this valley. "Come on."

She dashed to the stall; I had to run to keep up. It was a simple structure with bamboo walls and thatched roof. Inside, Cloud stood quietly, her rear foot raised. Her knee was swollen but not badly.

Lana offered the horse a piece of sugarcane. Cloud sniffed it but would not take it.

"She is still weak," Lana said, caressing the horse's long, beautiful face. "But she will be OK. Won't you, girl?"

Cloud whinnied softly.

The horse was big and handsome, pure milky white except for a light sprinkling of smoky gray along her back. She was well named.

"Do you ride her much?" I asked.

"Oh, yes!" Lana looked at me with shining eyes. "When she is better we will both ride her. Because you saved her. You are our friend always. Isn't he, Cloud?"

The horse bobbed her head and neighed, and we couldn't help but laugh.

8

For lunch we ate *poi*, a gooey white pudding Lana had made from taro root. She showed me how to stick a finger into it, twirl it around, then slurp the *poi* off. It didn't have much flavor.

"This is ancient Hawaiian food," she told me. "Grandfather said it is the only food a person really needs."

"Tastes kind of like mashed potatoes," I said.

"But potato is sweet."

"I mean Irish potatoes. You know."

She shook her head questioningly.

"It's a white potato, not sweet. This is kind of like mashed potatoes would be if they were sticky." I didn't tell her that I liked mashed potatoes better.

After lunch we napped, lying in our separate rooms while insects murmured outside. I woke when I heard Lana stirring. She was taking some kind of spear down from the wall in the main room.

I sat up. "What are you doing?"

"Going fishing. Want to come?"

"Sure!"

Outside in the sunlight I saw she held a three-pronged gig with a cane handle, about as long as she was. She also carried her basket, which she stopped to line with grass as she led the way to the stream.

Even though she was barefoot, the rocky ground didn't bother her. And despite the baggy, funny-looking clothes, she looked as graceful as a deer. Her glossy black hair hung all the way down her back.

We passed the cemetery but she didn't glance over. I suspected it hurt too much to think about.

The jungle was so dark compared to the bright sunlight that at first I could barely see. But my eyes soon adjusted as we followed the clear, shallow stream, which flowed over black rocks.

Lana paused and whispered, "Right up here is a good place." Setting the basket down, she crept to the edge of the pool and stepped in. I watched from the bank. She waded up to her waist and stopped. Staring into the water, she raised her gig and froze.

Suddenly she threw. The spear plunged into the water, and when Lana yanked it up a small fish was

wriggling on the barbs. Pulling the fish off, she tossed it onto the bank, and I put it in the basket.

In half an hour Lana had ten fish, none bigger than my hand. Then she lay the gig down and waded to the deep end of the pool, where the roots of tall trees reached down into the water. Feeling with her feet, she ducked to her chin and grabbed something off the bottom. She held up a tiny creature.

"Shrimp," she said.

"I thought they lived in the ocean."

"Freshwater shrimp." She tossed it to me, then repeated the process. Soon we had a dozen.

"Want to try?" Lana asked me.

"Sure."

"Take off your shoes."

Barefoot, I waded into the pool, which was so cold it took my breath away.

"Feel around with your toes. They'll prick at you. Then grab them," she explained.

It felt creepy to stick my feet among the roots. I kept expecting a snapping turtle or something to grab me. When a shrimp stabbed me I pulled back with a gasp.

Lana laughed. "They won't hurt you. Do it again, then grab them while they are fighting your toes."

I tried again. When I felt a nibble I laughed, since it tickled. Then I reached down, but got only a pebble. It took several tries before my fingers wrapped around a lively little shrimp. I held it up.

"Got one!"

"Great!" she said. "That's a good one. Give it here and I'll put it in the basket."

She took it and snapped its neck with her thumb.

"Want me to catch more?" I asked.

"Whatever you want. We have enough for supper."

"I'm coming out, then. This water's cold."

We waded out. Our wet clothes felt good in the hot, humid jungle.

On the way back Lana detoured into a thicket to pick guavas, adding them to the basket. We snacked on the fruit as we went along. Suddenly we heard a grunt and a crash.

"Hogs!" Lana shouted.

A herd of them vanished noisily into the shadows.

"I wish I had the gun," she said.

Then something moved in the dry leaves to my right, some kind of reptile.

"Is that a snake?" I said, remembering the cobras.

"Lizard," she said. "We've got enough food or I'd catch him. But we should be careful. There may be more snakes. I keep forgetting because there's never been any here before."

"Really! We don't want to run into another one."

"I just don't understand how that thing got here," Lana said. "Grandmother always told me Hawaii was famous for not having any snakes. I'd never even seen one until yesterday."

"You know, I remember reading that snakes got on the island of Guam," I said. "They just took over because there weren't any predators. Now there's, like, millions."

Lana stopped and stared at me with concern. "Really? Millions?"

I nodded. "They're everywhere."

"Oh, Eric! You don't think that could happen here? Not in Bamboo Bay!"

9

The thought of cobras on the loose took the pleasure out of walking. We watched the ground with every footstep.

When we reached the clearing with the cemetery, Lana took my hand. "Come. I will show you my family's graves," she said softly.

She led me to the four wooden markers.

"My parents died in a *tsunami* when I was a baby," Lana said.

"In a what?"

"Tidal wave. Grandfather said it is the only thing bad about our valley. When Pele becomes angry she pours fire from the mountains, or makes the earth shake, or sends *tsunami* from the sea. I was a baby and don't remember. Grandfather said he and Grandmother were in the house with me when they heard the wave coming. My parents were out at sea, fishing. My grandparents carried me to high ground before the wave hit, but we never saw my parents again. My grandmother put up these crosses to remember them. Then, when Grandmother died, Grandfather honored her by putting a cross here. And when Grandfather died, I put one here for him."

She caressed the rough wood of the cross gently. A tear came to her eye. I put a hand on her shoulder.

"I'm sorry, Lana," I said as she began to cry. "I'm so sorry."

She rested her head on my shoulder and I put my arm around her. It struck me how lonely she must feel. She could be tough and strong, but she needed a shoulder to cry on, just like anybody would.

"If not for you, I would have lost Cloud, my last friend on earth," Lana said.

Not knowing what to say, I just stood quietly beside her.

After a while she quit crying and dabbed her face with her shirt. As she stooped to pick up the basket, I noticed something odd at the edge of the clearing.

"Just a minute," I said.

While she waited I went over and found a short-handled shovel.

"You left your shovel over here," I said, holding it up. Then I noticed a bundle of young plants wrapped in burlap. They appeared to be nearly dead.

"That is not my shovel," Lana said, joining me.

"These aren't your plants?"

She knelt and examined a leaf. "I have never seen this kind of plant before."

I bent over. It had five pointed fronds with jagged edges. It looked familiar somehow. Then I remembered the plant from drug-education class. "That's marijuana!"

"Mari-what?" she said.

"Marijuana! A drug!" My mind raced. Those backpackers must have left it. I remembered now how the man acted funny when Todd asked if he planned to call the police.

"What is it?" Lana asked, studying my face. "What's the matter?"

"Those two campers yesterday. Were they acting suspicious?"

"I saw them near the cemetery," she said. "When they camped on the beach, I didn't like it, but OK, I let them. But then they came snooping up here. That's when I shot near them, to warn them away."

"I get it now," I said. "They came in here to plant marijuana. That's an illegal drug, Lana. It's against the law to grow it. People like to plant it in remote areas. They hope no one will find it, and even if somebody does, there won't be any way to tie it to them since it's on public land. They can come and check on it while pretending to be ordinary campers."

Thunder rumbled as a black cloud covered the sun. A cool wind gusted across the valley.

I knew now that the hiker didn't call the police like he said he would. But I was positive my parents would have, once Todd got home and told them I'd gone to investigate gunshots. Again, I wondered what would happen to Lana when the officials arrived.

"Come on," Lana said. "Before it rains."

She led the way, and we made it to the house just before the storm hit. It came all of a sudden, a massive downpour that hid the world behind a gray screen. We sat cross-legged on the floor watching water gush off the thatched eaves. I imagined the trail I'd come down the day before turning to mud. Probably can't get out of the valley now anyway, I thought—happily, I admit.

I yawned, forgetting the marijuana growers. They were gone now anyway. All my problems seemed far, far away . . .

I woke to music. It was a gentle sound, as sweet as the last of the rain that tinkled off the roof into puddles. As my eyes focused I saw my Hawaiian friend sitting against the wall playing a bamboo flute.

The sound was haunting, like musical owls. Insects murmured quietly around the house. The rain filled the air with lush smells. Outside, a ray of sunlight broke through the drizzle, painting a green-gold streak across the mountainside. Then it touched the waterfall, which turned to liquid fire pouring into a pool of pure light. And all the time Lana gently played.

I had never felt more peaceful in my life.

10

After the rain ended we checked on Cloud. She seemed better, but Lana was concerned about the ugly wound on her ankle. Leaving me to pet the horse, she hurried into the jungle and returned with a handful of leaves, which she wrapped around the leg and tied in place with a vine.

"That will keep it from getting infected," Lana said. "I don't want to let her out yet. She needs to stay off it."

We collected armfuls of grass and lay them in the stall, where Cloud munched hungrily. Lana replenished her water trough with a bucket from the pool by the waterfall.

It was late in the afternoon. The clouds had broken up, leaving a patchy blue sky. The sun had dropped behind the high ridge.

In the center of the main room in the house was a large square of tin covered with sand and ashes and ringed with stones. Lana fetched some dry leaves and twigs from a woodpile under the house. Then she struck flint against steel, sending sparks into the leaves, which began to smoke. Lana blew on them until a puff of flame appeared, then she added twigs. I got more wood from under the house and stoked the fire. Then from my pack I took the lighter I'd brought to make campfires.

"Look," I said, flicking it to show Lana how it worked. "Take this. It will make your job easier from now on."

"Does it last forever?"

"No. It'll run out."

She smiled. "Then I'll stay with my way."

"But this is easier!"

"Yes. And then it will run out, and my way will seem hard."

I thought about it, then chuckled. "You're right. I hadn't thought of that."

"When my grandmother was alive, she never let the fire go out," Lana said, fanning the flames with a large leaf to keep it going. "She was always near the house. But I am gone too often for that."

She stood. "I will go clean the fish. You tend the fire."

She took the basket and went out. When she returned I was still adding sticks.

"That's enough," she said. "Now we let it die down to coals, then we can cook."

She fetched a pot from a shelf on the wall and filled it from the bucket outside. Then she brought in some banana leaves and arranged them on the floor like a tablecloth. After the fire flickered down, she lay a metal grill over the embers and placed the fish on it. In a few minutes they darkened. Using a cloth for a mitt, Lana set the grill on the banana leaves, then put the shrimp in the pot and placed it over the coals.

I was impressed by how efficiently she did everything. I was also struck by how much work was involved, especially with no running water or electricity!

Lana pointed to the fish. "We can eat these now, and then the shrimp will be ready."

"Great!" I bowed my head and said a silent prayer of thanks. When I looked up she was watching me curiously.

"That is a prayer?" she asked.

"Yes."

Her eyes grew wistful. "My grandmother used to pray before we ate. Let me see if I can remember."

She closed her eyes. "God is great, God is good. Let us thank him for our food." She paused.

"By his hands," I prompted.

She nodded. "By his hands, we are fed, give us, Lord, our daily bread."

"Amen."

"Amen," she said, opening her eyes with a smile. "I was very small when I learned that." Then the smile faded. "Grandfather never prayed."

She reached for a fish, peeling the skin back to reveal white flesh. I did the same, eating with my fingers. It was delicious, though I wished we had salt.

By the time we finished, water was bubbling in the pot. Lana let it cook for a few minutes before taking it off the heat. She poured the steaming water out the door, then dumped the pink shrimp onto the banana leaves. After they cooled, we peeled them and popped them into our mouths. They were plump, firm, and tender.

"All we need is cocktail sauce," I said.

"What is that?"

"A sauce made from tomatoes and stuff. It's kind of tangy and salty."

"Sometimes when I crave salt I cook in seawater."

"Sounds smart!"

"Are you still hungry? I can bake breadfruit," she offered.

"I'm full, thanks."

"Tomorrow we will have some. It is almost as good as *poi*."

She rose and patted her belly. "I am happy now. Plenty of food. No more hikers. Cloud is doing well." She stepped to the door and peered out at the twilight. "Also, there is a full moon."

She turned and smiled at me, her white teeth gleaming. "Wait here." She crossed the room and entered her bedroom. A few moments later she came out wearing a knee-length white T-shirt belted at the waist.

"Tonight we visit the humpbacks," she said.

"The humpbacks? What are you talking about?"

"I mean tonight we swim with the whales. Come on."

11

I didn't believe her, not even when she set off down the path toward the sea. I gave her my flashlight so we wouldn't step on snakes, but she turned it off when we reached the shore. A full yellow moon halfway up the sky showed choppy waves rolling in from the open Pacific. The cliffs on either side of us were bathed in blond light.

She set the flashlight down and waded into the water, which sloshed around her.

"Come on!" she said.

"Are you crazy?" I said, but she was already swimming out to sea.

Skeptical and confused, I kicked off my shoes and socks, stripped off my shirt and picked my way over the big rocks to the water. Wading to my knees, I plunged in. It was cold and lively, sucking and churning around me. It was kind of scary. But I saw Lana's head farther out and stroked toward her.

Wait a minute. Was I losing my mind? Paddling out to sea at night, to swim with so-called whales?

It wasn't much fun either, with salty waves splashing over my head, getting in my eyes and nose, making me cough, tossing me up and down.

"It gets smoother farther out," Lana said. I saw her just a few yards away, waiting for me. Her presence reassured me.

Then she resumed swimming. As with everything she did, her movements were strong and relaxed. She was as graceful in water as on land.

"There aren't really any whales out here, are there?" I called after her, but she didn't answer.

There was nothing to do but swim. If I went back to shore I would be a wimp. If she could do it, so could I. The trick was to stay calm and not get spooked by the waves. It couldn't be as dangerous as it seemed or she wouldn't be doing it. Right?

So I swam. And swam. The water did get better farther out, rising in big smooth swells instead of choppy waves. Every so often I checked to make sure I could see Lana. She stayed just ahead, stroking steadily.

My arms were starting to get tired. I needed to rest.

"Lana!" I called.

She turned and paddled back to me.

"I'm tired," I said, trying not to sound whiny.

"Float on your back, like this." She stretched her arms out over her head and lay back. "Just kick your feet sometimes and you'll stay up."

Sure, I knew that. I tried it. It was almost as good as resting on dry land. We lay side by side on our backs in the water.

"I love it out here," Lana said.

"You don't get tired?"

"Not really. I just rest like this."

"You're not afraid?"

"Of what?"

"You know, sea creatures."

Just then, over the slosh of the waves, I heard a long, hissing noise.

"Like that?" she said.

We spun around. Two geysers of silvery spray spurted into the air.

"They're here!" Lana cried joyfully.

"No way," I said. "Whales? For real?"

The geysers disappeared. The dark forms beneath them melted away.

"That was some kind of surf or something, wasn't it?" I said.

I looked at Lana to see what she would say. Suddenly, as if she had sprouted wings, she rose straight up onto the air. It took me a moment to realize that a

huge, black whale had come up underneath her, lifting her high on its back.

"Lana!" I yelled. "Lanaaaaaaaa—" Something came up under me, something as big as a house, and I rose so fast my stomach flip-flopped.

"Over here!" she shouted.

I toppled over, but the whale's back was so broad I didn't fall off.

Lana had gotten to her feet and was standing shakily, her arms spread for balance. In the darkness I couldn't make out many details about the creatures, just their black shapes and strange slurpy sounds.

When I realized the whale wasn't about to drop me, I got to my feet too, feeling its slippery smooth skin like warm vinyl against my soles.

"I'm doing it!" I shouted. "I'm standing!"

"Great, Eric!" Lana said.

Then the whale began to sink like a Ferris wheel, slowly, gently, and I was left bobbing in the water. Lana's animal did the same, as if the two were acting together. They vanished beneath us.

"Isn't it wonderful?" she said.

"This can't be happening," I said. "It's got to be a hallucination. Maybe handling that marijuana. Whoooaaa!" I yelled as we went up again.

Our whales were side by side now. We were just a few yards away on their backs. We could almost reach out and touch hands. This time I got to my feet more easily.

"Hang on," Lana said. "I think we're going to ride."

The whales lurched forward, dropped a bit, then began surging across the sea. We started out slow but picked up speed—incredible speed—faster than a ski boat, headed straight out to sea.

"Uh, Lana?" I said.

She didn't hear me.

"Lana!"

"What?"

"Aren't we, like, going the wrong way?"

She laughed. "Just wait, Eric! We've just begun!"

12

For hours we rode during the most incredible night of my life. The whales took us miles out to sea, far out of sight of land. Then, as if tired, the whales set us down gently in the water and submerged. I started to worry, but Lana just laughed and told me to be patient. Sure enough, they surfaced, picking us up again like we were their pets.

I realized this was like surfing—whale surfing! I was catching a wave at last. I held my arms out and sang "Surfin' Safari," to myself at first, then out loud.

"What's that?" Lana asked when I finished.

"A surfing song. Old-time rock 'n' roll."

"Here's a song my grandmother taught me." She began to sing in Hawaiian, waving her arms and twisting slowly in some kind of hula dance. The song was so pretty it gave me chills.

"Beautiful!" I said when she finished.

"Grandmother said it is a very old song, one her mother taught her."

The whales swam on and on under the moon and stars. Once, they dropped us off and swam beside us, making funny noises: coos, whistles, and clicks. There were just two, one for each of us, and we stroked their sides and fins. They were so huge!

Then we both climbed on the same whale, while the other cavorted beside us. We held hands for better balance, standing side by side on the big, smooth platform of its back, zooming across the endless Pacific in the silvery light. Lana's T-shirt glowed like an angel's dress, her eyes sparkling.

Resting, we sat side by side on the whale's back as if we were on the bow of a speedboat, the salt spray in our faces, the other whale gliding beside us. Lana's long black hair streamed behind her. When she looked at me she smiled and her face glowed in the moonlight.

"I don't ever want to stop," I told her. "I'd like to ride forever."

"Me too."

"Maybe we could get them to take us to some other island where nobody lives and we could stay there."

"You don't like Bamboo Bay?"

"Yes, but I mean, it's been discovered. I mean an island that nobody knows about."

"I would be homesick. Let's stay at Bamboo Bay."

"Just us?"

"And Cloud."

I laughed. "I'm sorry. I forgot about Cloud. Maybe we could go back and get her."

"She wouldn't like this."

"Sure she would!" I said. "She could ride the other whale there. And we could take turns riding *her*. Wouldn't that be cool!"

Lana laughed. "You have a wild imagination, Eric."

"Let me tell you something, Lana. My imagination isn't half as wild as what's really happening!"

We both laughed.

Again the whales dropped us off far out at sea and vanished, but I didn't worry, even though we might be halfway to China by now. We swam in the big, gentle swells, and floated on our backs when we got tired. Soon the humpbacks returned. We climbed onto one and headed back the way we'd come.

"Why do you think they do this?" I asked Lana.

"The whales? Because they love us."

"But why do they love us?"

"Because we love them. Don't you?"

"Yes. Definitely."

"I do too. They can feel our love. And we can feel theirs. Listen." She lay on her side and put her ear to the whale's back. "You can hear the heartbeat."

"No way!" But I put my ear down and, sure enough, far beneath me in the great animal I heard a deep pulse like a distant kettledrum. "Cool!"

We lay side by side, facing each other, listening to the whale's thundering heart.

The humpback slowed to an easy cruise and we explored its back—the giant blowhole, the long spine, the dorsal fin. The creature seemed to want to cooperate, keeping its back above the water for us. When we reached the huge tail, the rest of the body dipped under and the tail elevated like a double-wide diving board.

"Come on," Lana said, tugging my hand.

We stepped up cautiously one on each fluke.

"Let's dive," she said.

"You first." I was chicken.

Suddenly the whale flicked its tail, launching us into the air. I went up and up, my arms and legs flailing. From the corner of my eye I saw Lana put her hands together for a perfect dive. I wasn't so graceful.

"Whoooaa!" I yelled as I began to fall, rear end first. I straightened my legs and pinched my nose shut just before I hit. I knifed into the cold black water, down and down. Finally I slowed, kicked my legs, and began floating up. All around me I heard whale noises, hums and peeps and cheerful moans. When I popped up, Lana was treading water nearby. I saw that we weren't far from the cliffs of Bamboo Bay.

"See?" she said, her face glowing. "Isn't it great?"

"Definitely." My whole body tingled with excitement. "Do you do this often?"

"They usually come when the moon is full. Sometimes I swim out and they're not there, and I just swim back, no problem. Other times, though, we do this."

"Did you go with your grandfather?"

"No. He was too old. I've always gone alone—until now."

"Is it always just two?"

"Oh no! Sometimes there's a whole pod, and they take turns letting me ride."

I looked around for the whales but didn't see them. We moved our arms back and forth to stay afloat, expecting them at any moment. But they didn't show.

"Will they be back?" I asked Lana.

As if in answer, the whales spouted as they moved out toward deep sea.

"Good-bye!" Lana shouted. "Aloha!"

"Aloha!" I called.

We turned and swam toward shore.

13

We were so exhausted we didn't even try to make it to the house. We picked our way over the rocks and collapsed on the ground just beyond, instantly falling asleep.

We didn't wake till the morning sun warmed us. We rose, stretched—and grinned at the sight of each other. Our hair was tangled and our clothes filthy from lying on the ground.

We walked back to the house, and the first thing Lana wanted to do was check on Cloud. We found the horse moving around in her stall, eager to get out. Lana hugged her neck.

"I'm so glad you're better," she said.

Removing the poultice, she led the white horse out of the stall. Cloud pranced a few steps, showing only the slightest limp.

"Soon we'll be able to ride!" Lana told me happily. Then she looked down at her dirt-smeared T-shirt. "I think I need a bath."

We took turns bathing and washing our clothes in the pool. When she finished I had a breakfast of fresh fruit laid out for us.

We were just sitting down to eat when a shadow darkened the doorway. A man dressed in camouflage stepped in holding a pistol! At first I thought he was a member of a SWAT team, but something about his manner told me otherwise.

"All right," he barked. "Where's the dude with the gun?"

Lana gasped. "Who are you?"

I saw he was wearing stiff brown leggings from knee to ankle. It was the backpacker, George, the man Todd and I had met when we hiked in!

"Don't worry about who I am, little lady," he said in a menacing voice. "I asked you a question." Then he stared at me. "Say, aren't you the kid I saw on the trail?"

"Yes, sir."

"What are you doing here? I thought you were leaving."

"I came down to see what was the matter."

"Yeah? And what did you find out?"

I debated what to tell him. If I told him the truth, that there was no gunman, he would know we were unprotected. If I lied and said we were expecting somebody, like Lana's father, he would hold us hostage. And when he found out the truth he would really be angry.

"There was no gunman," I said.

"Don't lie to me, kid! I heard the shots."

"It was her. She was trying to run people off because this is her valley."

"So where's your old man?" he demanded of Lana. "Don't tell me you live here alone." I saw anger and sorrow cross Lana's face.

"Her parents are dead," I answered. "She lived here with her grandfather, but he died recently, and she's been here ever since."

He frowned, unsure whether to believe me.

"Look," I said. "Do you think I'd be down here if there really had been a gunman? I found the girl and took her rifle away. There's nobody else."

"So why are you still here?"

That was one question I couldn't answer. Lana spoke up. "My horse was snakebit," she said. "He saved her. He stayed to make sure she was all right."

"Snakebit? There aren't any snakes in Hawaii," George said.

"Then why are you wearing those?" I said, pointing at his leggings.

He looked down at them and frowned, trying to come up with an answer. Then he laughed. "Caught me red-handed, huh? That's what you think."

"Yes," I said. The pieces of the puzzle were coming together all of a sudden. "It was you who left the marijuana and the shovel. You came in here to plant it, and you released the cobra to protect your crop. That's why you're wearing snakeproof leggings."

"So we've got a Sherlock Holmes here, do we?" he said. "Well, maybe that dope was mine and maybe it wasn't. You've got no proof either way. I'm just an innocent backpacker, see? I was hiking in with my lady and this crazy girl takes potshots at us. So we hightailed it, and today I came around in my boat. As for the snake, maybe I'd heard there were cobras in this valley, and that's why I wear leggings."

"She's lived here all her life and there's never been any before," I argued.

"Yeah? Well, even if it was my snake, that doesn't tie me to the marijuana."

"Bringing snakes into Hawaii is a major offense, a federal wildlife violation," I said. "The marijuana charge is probably minor in comparison."

"Destroying somebody else's property is against the law too, ever thought of that? I take it you killed my snake—if it *was* my snake. Who gave you the right?"

"Are you kidding? You turn a deadly snake loose in a valley where somebody lives? Suppose she had been bitten?" The thought made me angry.

"Hey, I didn't know anybody lived here, all right?" he said. "I just read in the paper about this new park. Sure, I noticed that little cemetery, but I figured it was from ancient times. I never even saw the house or garden. Little Annie Oakley here opened fire on me before I got a chance."

He stared at us, and his gaze made me shiver. The danger of our situation suddenly hit me—Lana and me alone in the remote valley with an armed criminal.

"Besides," he said, "I figured something like this might happen to my cobra, once I realized somebody was back here. So I've got the solution. Come on." He waved the pistol at us. We got up and went outside.

On the ground were two burlap sacks tied with cord. George untied each of them. Grabbing the bottom ends of the sacks, he tugged them gently until they came open. Two long cobras slithered out, testing the air with their tongues.

"Yep, I've solved the problem this time," George said. "That's a male and a female. Soon there'll be dozens of baby cobras, and I can grow all the dope I want with nobody bothering me."

Side by side the snakes moved rapidly across the ground and vanished into deep grass.

14

"Let's go for a little boat ride, kids," George growled.

Keeping the gun pointed at us, he marched us down the path, into the jungle, and along the creek to the shore. At the far end of the bay, a small outboard motorboat lay on a narrow strip of black sand.

"Where are we going?" Lana asked. I could hear the fear in her voice.

"Just get in."

She stepped into the open boat and I followed. George pushed the vessel out into the rough water, hopped in, and quickly started the motor. Sitting at the steering wheel, he backed the boat up, turned it around and headed into the waves. Soon we were out of Bamboo Bay and clipping across the tops of the breakers, straight toward deep sea.

"My friend Todd was going to call the police," I said desperately. "They could be here any time."

"Bull. Your friend has had plenty of time to call the cops. Either he forgot about you or something happened to him. Maybe my snake bit him on the way out." He laughed.

Lana seemed lost in thought—or terror. My heart beat faster as I realized there was no escape. We were defenseless.

When the island was a tiny speck behind us, the bearded man cut the motor down to idle. Ocean swells tossed the small vessel up and down. He reached for a rope and grabbed my arm.

"Wait!" I said. "If you tie us and somebody finds us, they'll know we've been murdered."

He frowned, then nodded. "You're right." Gazing back to shore, he said, "You'll never make it back from here anyway."

A large wave slapped the boat, knocking Lana off her feet. She tumbled into the stern and must have hit her head, because she lay there for several moments, as if dazed.

"What's the matter back there?" George demanded. "Come on, you!"

He took her arm roughly and yanked her to her feet. She screamed as he tried to push her overboard.

"Hey! Leave her alone!" I yelled, grabbing hold of Lana to steady her. But he slugged me in the stomach, and next thing I knew I was falling over the side of the boat, Lana with me.

"Give my regards to King Neptune," George said, revving the motor. The boat left us in its wake as it headed back to the island.

"Hold onto my hand!" Lana called, reaching for me in the churning waves.

I grabbed her fingers but a surge pulled us apart.

"Lana!" I shouted. In just seconds she was yards away.

"Swim for the island!" she said, her voice faint.

I slipped down in the trough of a swell, and when I came up I couldn't see her anywhere. I tried not to panic, I just aimed for where I thought the shore should be, and swam.

The trouble was, I couldn't see land. I waited till I reached a crest, then jumped as high as I could. In the distance I saw a mountain peak.

I tried not to think of the miles that lay between me and it. One thing was sure: The distance was greater than I had ever swum in my life!

If the water were calm, my chances would be better. But this felt like a washing machine in the agitate cycle. I was constantly bobbing up and down. Waves sloshed into my face. Even the wind seemed against me. I started to feel nauseous—and very afraid.

"Lana!" I yelled again.

Nothing.

Panic gripped me. Then I remembered floating on my back last night when I got tired. I tried it now, but kept getting water in my face. It was like the ocean wanted to kill me!

"God, please get us out of this," I prayed. "Get us safely to land. Bless Lana and keep her safe. In Jesus' name, amen."

I felt better. My heart didn't race so fast. I could do this. If I just took my time and swam, stroke after stroke, and rested when I was tired, I could make it.

I swam. And swam.

Every so often I rode to the top of a high crest to catch a glimpse of the mountaintop. It didn't seem to get any closer. I tried to stay calm, and just kept paddling.

My joints were getting sore, and my muscles. And I was cold! This might be the tropics, but the Pacific Ocean felt chilly! I tried not to think of how deep the water was—or what might live in it.

I rested on my back. Then swam. Then rested. I was running out of energy, and for some reason I was getting sleepy. I had read how Arctic explorers, when dying from the cold, simply fell asleep and never woke up. Was that what it would be like out here? Would I just doze off, and not wake up until my lungs were full of brine?

The thoughts terrified me, but I felt too tired to stay frightened. I wanted to sleep—just a short nap, that's all. When I floated on my back I could nap for a few seconds, but then I began to sink and water got in my face, waking me. I kept trying, and kept waking up.

Finally I could take no more. I had to sleep, whatever the cost. I stretched out and closed my eyes.

As if in a fever, I began to dream I was lying in my bed. Lana knelt at my head, caressing me gently. When I looked up into her face, she smiled sweetly.

"I'm so glad you've come," I told her.

Then I realized I was really talking, and she was really here. This was no dream! I sat up to discover my "bed" was a whale's back!

"Eric! Eric!" Lana cried, shaking me. "The whale found us! I saw you floating on your back. You were going down. Then we came up under you—and you didn't even wake up!"

I was so happy to be alive I hugged her.

"Where's the other whale?" I asked.

Suddenly it broke the surface, spouting, and made a loud belching noise. Lana and I giggled.

"We're close now," she said, pointing.

I spun around and saw the cliffs of Bamboo Bay looming dead ahead.

"Thank you, Jesus!" I said.

Lana added, "Yes, thank you!"

15

From the shore we waved as the whales headed back out to sea.

"They won't be back for another month," Lana said.

"I wonder where they go."

"Who knows? Maybe down the coast to other parts of the island. Maybe to other islands. Or maybe across the sea."

"I'm sure glad they found us."

She nodded. "I think if that man had not carried us so far out, perhaps they would not have."

The memory of the guy made me grit my teeth. "It makes me so mad he would try something like that." I shook my head. "He's probably all the way back to Hilo by now, safe and sound."

"Oh, I don't think so."

"What do you mean?"

She reached into the pocket of her shorts and pulled out a small, round object—the boat plug!

"Lana!" I hugged her so hard she giggled. "You're the greatest! How did you even know about a boat plug?"

"I noticed it when we were going out. I figured that's what it was for, to let the water out when the boat is on dry land. So when we stopped I pretended to fall down and hit my head so I could remove it."

"You could be a secret agent for sure!"

"What is a 'secret agent'?"

I laughed. "I'll tell you later. Come on." I took her hand and we headed up the path through the jungle. The valley had never looked so beautiful—until I remembered the cobras.

"What are we going to do about the snakes?" I asked.

"I don't know," Lana said sadly, "except that I have been praying very hard."

"You? Pray? I thought you didn't do that."

"When I saw you pray it made me happy inside. I wanted to do that. And it made me feel better."

"It's not magic, you know."

"I know. But it helps, don't you think?"

"Definitely!"

We left the stream, passed the cemetery, then the waterfall. Up near the house I detected movement—dark forms milling around, grunting noises.

"Hogs!" Lana cried. "They must have been in the garden! Oh, I wish I had my gun!"

"But look," I said. "They're by the house."

She frowned. "That is very strange. I have never seen them come so close."

"Come on, let's check it out."

We ran toward the house. Though the hogs were usually wary of humans, they hardly noticed us. They were in a frenzy about something. When we were several yards away, I grabbed Lana's arm.

"Wait," I said. "They might hurt us if we come closer."

There were about a dozen black, bristly beasts, some with curved tusks. They milled around excitedly, grunting, squealing, churning up a cloud of dust.

"Look. One's down," I said. "It's as if they're attacking it."

"No!" Lana said. "They're not attacking the hog! They're attacking a snake!"

"Two snakes!" I said.

An incredible battle was taking place: the herd of hogs versus the two cobras. I remembered reading that pigs don't hesitate to attack snakes. Pioneers had liked having them around because they cleaned out the reptiles almost as if they hated them. But I also thought hogs were immune to venom, yet one was lying dead on the ground. That was probably an old folktale.

There was no question who was winning the battle. The cobras writhed with broken backs. Hogs rushed in, stomping, biting, and hooking them with their tusks, then danced out of the way before the fangs could strike. Soon the serpents were dead, but the hogs didn't stop. They continued to rip the reptiles to pieces.

"They are eating the snakes!" Lana said. Like me she seemed shocked but glad.

I was afraid the swine would turn on us, and I was prepared to step between them and Lana if they did. But they ignored us.

Finally not a trace remained of the snakes. The hogs calmed down, nosing around the dead one as if in mourning.

Suddenly a boar raised its head, as if noticing us for the first time. With a grunt it turned and fled, and the whole herd thundered after it, disappearing into the bushes.

Lana knelt beside the dead animal. "I'm so sorry," she said, touching its bristly side. "I'm sorry you had to die. I'm sorry I hunted you. I never will again. I'll build a fence around my garden. I'll . . ."

Abruptly she stood up and faced me. "No I won't," she said. "I won't build a fence, because I'm not going to stay here."

"You're not?"

"No. I know now it is no use. This valley is not mine anymore. I can't keep things the way they were. Those days are gone."

She looked around the beautiful valley—the green mountainsides, the tree-shaped bamboo house, the lush garden, the silvery waterfall tumbling into the pool. Tears welled up in her eyes.

"Eric," she said. "It is time for us to go."

16

Lana packed her few possessions into a cloth pillowcase—some utensils, clothes, a hairbrush given to her by her grandmother, her flute, plus some bananas for our trip. We loaded that plus my backpack on Cloud's back, deciding to walk beside her to spare her leg. I carried the rifle over my shoulder on a sling.

When we reached the cemetery, Lana asked for some time alone. I went to the edge of the meadow and sat on a large flat rock.

It wobbled under me, and when I adjusted it I heard a hollow sound. Curious, I lifted it and found a hole underneath. Peeking in, I saw a black book wrapped in plastic.

A Bible! It must be the one her grandfather hid, the one that had belonged to Lana's grandmother!

I opened the plastic bag and pulled the book out. It had a musty, library smell, but seemed in good condition. It was an old-time Bible, with a soft, black leather cover and thin, crinkly pages with gold edges. A red satin ribbon served as a bookmark, and the words of Jesus were in red.

I was reading one of my favorite verses, John 3:16, when Lana walked up. "What's that?" she asked.

I could tell by her voice she had been crying. I showed her the book. "Your grandmother's Bible," I said. "I found it under this rock."

She stared at it with tear-reddened eyes. Then she reached for it, hugged it to her chest, and silently wept. Cloud walked to her and nickered gently.

Lana dried her tears with a finger. "What were you reading?" she asked me.

I showed her the verse. She began to read, awkwardly. I recalled that she had not had much schooling.

"For God so loved the world, that he gave his only begotten Son, that who—that whosoever believeth in him should not—should not perish, but have everlasting life."

She looked at me. "Is that true?"

"Yes."

She closed the book thoughtfully. "I want to read more later." She put it back in the plastic bag carefully and into the pillowcase. "Are you ready?"

I nodded.

We entered the jungle and followed the stream, pausing when we got to the pool where she had gigged fish. "I see one now," she whispered, pointing. I could tell she longed to wade in and throw a spear, to feel for shrimp with her toes.

We continued down the stream to the hiking trail, which zigzagged up the mountainside. When we reached the bend with the view, we stopped to take a last look at the valley. Lana stood facing the blue bay, high cliffs, and lush valley below. With her long black hair, brown skin, and bare feet, she seemed to belong there.

At last she turned away with a sigh. "All right," she said, nodding.

We ascended the steep trail. Climbing the mountain didn't seem as difficult as it had when I hiked in. I also noticed my skin was darker. I must have gotten a pretty good tan during my stay.

We reached the top and the trail leveled off through the forest. Cloud's hooves made a gentle clip-clop on the soft earth behind us. Lana, barefoot, made no sound at all.

"Do you have any other family that you know of?" I asked.

"There was an aunt," she said. "After Grandmother died, Grandfather went over the mountain to find her. Later she came for a visit. But I never saw her again."

"So she doesn't know your grandfather is dead?"

"That's right."

"Do you know her name or where she lives?"

"All I remember is that I called her Aunt Iolani, and she lived somewhere in the islands; I don't know where."

We walked quietly for a while, listening to soft birdsong and the gentle breeze.

"Eric, what will happen to me when we get out?"

"We'll try to find your aunt or some family member. Maybe the ranchers who owned the valley will know more."

"I'm afraid, Eric."

"Why?"

"I know so little."

"So little? Lana, you know a lot. You know how to live off the land—how to raise taro and spear fish and catch shrimp and stuff."

"I thought everybody knew those things."

I laughed. "I don't know anybody who knows those things."

"Also, I don't have good clothes, and I won't know how to act."

"We'll get you some clothes. And you act just fine."

"I won't be as smart or pretty as other girls."

I stopped and grabbed her hands. "Would you knock it off? You're smarter and prettier than any girl."

"Really?"

"Really."

She smiled, and I knew then why time stood still in the valley. It was because of Lana.

"I will always remember our time together, Eric."

"It's not over yet, is it?"

"Our time together is not. But our time in the valley is, I'm afraid."

Her eyes were dark and liquid. As I stared into them, everything disappeared but Lana. I didn't hear the birds sing, smell the rain forest, or feel the breeze. All I knew was her.

Then Cloud whinnied and bobbed her head impatiently.

"She wants to go," Lana said, giggling.

I nodded reluctantly. "I guess we'd better."

"What will we do at the end of the trail?" she asked as we resumed walking.

"Heck, I don't know. I guess go to the highway and try to flag down a car. Or else walk to the nearest town. And that may be miles. I still can't figure out what happened to Todd."

She grabbed my hand. "Eric, look!" she whispered. "There's someone camped by the trail."

Up ahead in a pine grove stood a bright blue tent. As we approached I saw someone sitting outside against a tree—a boy, brown-haired, about sixteen.

"I don't believe it!" I said. "Todd?"

17

"Eric! I thought you were dead!"

"What are you doing camping here?" I asked as we hurried over.

"Can't you see?" He pointed to his outstretched left leg, swollen and bruised. "I broke my ankle, or sprained it. I stopped to pick some apples." He looked up at the limbs overhead. I recognized this as the same grove where we stopped before. "I got all I could get from the ground, so I climbed a tree. The branch broke and I landed wrong."

"Man!"

"I kept waiting for you, but when you didn't show up I was able to pitch the tent and get inside.

I've been here ever since, waiting for somebody to come by."

"It's a good thing you had food," I said.

"And aspirin!" He frowned as he shifted his weight. "But what happened to you? I figured you had gotten captured or shot by that crazy guy in the valley."

I laughed. "Todd, I'd like to introduce you to Lana. She's that 'crazy guy.'"

Lana smiled shyly as he stared in surprise.

"It's a long story," I said. "Her grandfather died and she felt like that was her valley and she decided to run everybody off. I managed to take the rifle away—it wasn't easy, either—and I stayed down there. I kept expecting *you*."

"Our parents don't expect us back till tomorrow night, so they wouldn't have any reason to come looking," Todd said. "What about those two people we saw hiking out? I thought they were going to call the police."

Lana and I glanced at each other. "That's a *really* long story, Todd. I'll tell you when we get out of here. For now we'd better load up and go. We'll put you on this horse, OK?"

"I'll do anything to get out of here. I've been dying of boredom—and worry. I didn't know *what* happened to you, dude!"

I took Todd's tent down and got his pack ready. Since mine was lighter, Lana agreed to carry it, and

I took Todd's. We left the pillowcase on Cloud. It wasn't easy getting Todd onto the horse, but finally he was in position, his left leg stuck out. He carried the rifle since it wouldn't fit on my shoulder with the pack strap.

It was late afternoon when we finally made it to the parking lot. Boy, was I glad to see that old truck! Lana and I removed our packs and helped Todd off the horse. He laid the rifle down and held onto my shoulder as he hobbled to the truck. He was unlocking the door when we heard a movement in the bed of the pickup. I glanced back just in time to see a man rise up, holding a knife.

"You!" I said, shocked to see George. He looked bedraggled and mean.

"You!" he said, even more surprised to see me.

He sprang out of the truck. He was barefoot, and several buttons were torn off his camouflage shirt. "You took that boat plug, didn't you, you little punk?" he said. "My boat sank about a mile offshore. I had to swim for it, and then I bushwhacked through the jungle till I finally found an old trail. I barely made it here with my life. But how did you get here?"

I shrugged. "You'll never believe me, but we rode a pair of whales."

George snarled. "I've had it with you kids! You've given me nothing but trouble! Now hand over the keys!"

"Sorry, George. There's three of us and only one of you," I said, edging toward the rifle.

He lunged. I jerked away but he managed to grab my wrist.

Next thing I knew he had me in close, the knife to my throat.

"All right, give me the keys," he said to Todd. "And stay away from that rifle or I'll cut his throat," he warned Lana.

Todd tossed George the keys, which he caught with his free hand.

"That's better," George said. "You twerps are all that stand between me and success, see? I finally came up with the perfect plan and you messed it up."

"What's so perfect about turning deadly snakes loose in my valley?" Lana demanded.

"Are you kidding? It's tropical, that's why. I tried using cobras at my patches in northern California, but they didn't do so good. Kept dying on me. They're from India and they like the heat. So I figured I'd move my operation here. It was dicey smuggling the snakes in, but after that there's been only one problem—you kids."

"Just let us go," Todd said. "We won't say anything."

Speak for yourself, I thought.

"Right, right," George said. "Tell you what. Girlie, you hand me that rifle, real easy, butt first. If you try anything, your boyfriend here will never see tomorrow."

"Don't do it, Lana!" I said. "Then he can kill us all!"

"Shut up!" George jammed the knife tight against my neck. I expected the blade to slit my throat at any second.

Suddenly Cloud, who had been standing behind Lana, bolted toward us. She reared up, pawing the air with her hooves just inches from our heads. Great! She was going to kill both of us! But George, terrified, loosened his grip, and I ducked free and ran. I turned just in time to see Cloud's front hoof knock the knife from his hand.

"All right, all right!" George yelled, diving under the truck. "Call it off!"

Lana whistled. "Here, Cloud. Here, girl."

The horse stood still, shaking her head as if warning George. I patted her neck. "Thank you, Cloud."

She whinnied and bobbed her head.

Lana grabbed the rifle and chambered a shell. Then she picked up the knife and stuck it in her belt.

"Got any rope?" I asked Todd, rubbing my neck.

"Behind the front seat."

I opened the door, leaned the seat forward, and pulled out a tangle of rope.

"Come on out," I told George. "She's got the gun, and as you recall, she's not shy about using it."

He crawled out in a hurry.

I took the keys from him, then tied his hands and feet together behind his back in the bed of the truck. I attached the end of the rope to the heavy spare tire lying nearby so he couldn't jump out.

"We're ready," I said. "Lana, you follow on the horse. Keep the gun, and if he gets loose, use it."

She nodded, then swung nimbly onto Cloud. Lana held the reins in her left hand with the rifle stock propped against her right thigh. The white horse pranced nervously, shaking her head. Lana quieted the big animal with a word.

Boy, she would be a good secret agent! I would have to tell Miss Spice about her.

I helped Todd get in on the passenger side.

"Eric, you've got to tell me what's going on," he said.

"I'll tell you when we get on the road," I said, sliding behind the steering wheel and putting the key in the ignition. "All right, let's move 'em out!"

Then I remembered something. "Uh, Todd? How do you drive this thing?"

18

Fortunately the truck had automatic transmis-
sion, so the only gears I had to learn were rever
and drive. But the big V–8 engine gave the veh
a lot of power, and it lurched every time I tou
the gas pedal. After a couple of false sta
reached the highway.

"Where's the nearest town, one with a
tion and a hospital?" I asked Todd.

"Take a left."

I turned onto the two-lane highv
ily there was little traffic. I drove
Cloud to follow at a trot.

We didn't get far before a s'
over. I guess a twelve-year-

followed by an armed girl on a horse needed check-ing out. It took a while to explain things, but finally he said he figured nobody could make up a story like ours. He handcuffed George and put him in the back of the patrol car, then escorted us into town.

We left Todd at the emergency room and tethered Cloud in the grass by the police station parking lot. She grazed happily, no doubt hungry after the long trip. The trooper took George off to jail, and Lana and I wound up with an officer who made us tell the whole story. A newspaper photographer showed up, and we went outside for him to take our picture standing next to Cloud. Then the ranch-ers who owned the valley arrived.

The man and woman were about my parents' age, and dressed more like Texans than Hawaiians, with jeans and boots and big straw hats. The woman hugged Lana and said she remembered her as a baby.

"I had no idea your grandfather stayed in the val-ley," she told Lana. "The state officials said they explained everything to him, and we assumed he'd moved. I'm so sorry to hear that he passed on." She hugged Lana again.

"We'll keep your horse for you as long as you want us to," said the man, who had a weather-beat-en face and graying sideburns. "We've got plenty of here—and other horses to keep her company."

"And take this," the woman whispered, slipping a wad of money into Lana's hands. "You may need it."

Lana's eyes glistened with tears. "I can't take it, really."

The woman shook her head. "It's the least we can do."

Just then my parents arrived, along with Todd's mother and father. The police must have called them too. They hugged us and peppered us with questions, then we all went down to the hospital to see about Todd. The doctors said he would have to stay there overnight.

The police had released Lana to my parents' custody, so she went with us back to Todd's house. It was midnight when we arrived. Lana stayed in Todd's room and I slept on the living-room sofa.

The next day Mother and Todd's mom took Lan shopping. They were gone nearly all day. W' they got back I was shocked: Lana got her ha' short!

"I tried to talk her out of it, but she ; Mom said.

Lana stared at the floor, as if afrai' like it.

"She said she's tired of brushing Martha explained.

"Wow!" I said. "That's what ' Lana glanced up. "Do you

"Yes. You look totally modern." I had loved her hair when it was long, but I had to admit she was a knockout with it short.

She broke into a big smile. She was wearing turquoise shorts, white socks and cool tennis shoes, and a T-shirt with a picture of a man in a dugout canoe that said, "Hawaii Natural." Plus she had sacks of other clothes and stuff.

"I told her she's the prettiest girl in Hawaii," Mom said.

"She's what Todd would call a babe," Martha said with a chuckle.

Lana looked down bashfully but peeked at me with a happy grin.

That night the newspaper called to say a big hotel in Kona offered to put my family and Lana up free for a week. Mom and Dad agreed to extend our vacation since the rooms would have cost them thousands and they didn't want to miss out on a good deal.

The next day we said good-bye to Todd's family nd drove a rental car around the island toward ona, stopping to visit Todd on the way.

I can't believe you guys are getting a free hotel " he said, propped up in bed. "I wish I could go you."

'o too," I said.

"By the way, a TV crew came by this morning and interviewed me," he said. "They said they'll meet you guys in Kona."

"Todd's going to be famous," Dad joked.

"Yeah, all the girls will want his autograph," I teased.

We said good-bye and went on to Kona, a beautiful town by the beach. Blue sea, white sand, palm trees, high-rise hotels, and mountains graced the background.

The hotel was the fanciest I'd ever seen. We had a suite, with three adjoining rooms, and balconies that looked out on the ocean.

As soon as we checked in, the police called to say they had found Lana's aunt. She lived on Maui but was in California on business and couldn't get back for several days. The aunt was shocked to hear about Lana and her grandfather, police said. She wanted to bring Lana home to live with her.

The TV crew arrived, and we agreed to do the interview in the hotel lobby. There was a guy with the camera and lights, a woman with a big microphone, and a handsome anchorman in a cream-colored suit. Lana and I sat on a sofa while the anchorman perched in a chair and asked us questions. He was friendly and I enjoyed it, but Lana seemed nervous. Afterward I told her that's just the way it is out here in civilization.

The next morning we ate breakfast in one of the hotel's restaurants, which was bright with sunlight and looked out on the beach. When we were finishing up, a waitress came to the table and said, "Mr. Sterling? I have a long-distance phone call for you, from the mainland."

Dad went out into the lobby. Meanwhile Mom went to the ladies' room.

"I love your parents," Lana told me. "They're so cool." She had started using modern words.

I laughed. "I love my parents too, but cool is not the word I would use to describe them."

"Oh, but they are!" she insisted. "And your dad! I love his shoes!"

"Excuse me?"

"Grandfather used to have a pair just like that. He said he got them from an army surplus store, whatever that is. He wore them for years."

I shook my head in wonder. "Picture that. Old Dad, cool."

Just then Dad returned. He was still wearing those green shoes, and they did look kind of cool, come to think of it.

"It's for you, Eric," he said.

"Not another reporter."

He shook his head and smiled, and I went to the main desk.

"Hello?" I said.

"Eric? Hey, this is Miss Spice."

"Miss Spice? Wow! How did you find out where I was?"

She laughed. "Are you kidding? You're all over the news. I'm glad you didn't mention WSI, by the way. That was smart."

I hadn't even thought about it, to tell the truth.

"I just wanted to congratulate you," she said.

"Thanks. I really didn't do that much, though."

"Eric! You busted up one of the biggest drug rings on the Pacific Rim."

"I did?"

"They didn't tell you? They're called The Cobras, because they use cobras to guard their marijuana patches. You caught the ringleader, Eric."

"Wow!"

"Believe it or not, I'd thought about assigning the case to you kids, but I decided it would be too dangerous."

"It was dangerous all right," I said.

"It's not the drugs that concerned us," she said. "The DEA—Drug Enforcement Agency—can handle that. We were worried about the cobras. If those things got loose on Hawaii, it would be an ecological catastrophe! You and Wailana did a fine job. By the way, she's a darling, Eric. Is she as sharp as she looks on TV?"

"A million times sharper! Wait till I tell you everything she did!"

"I can't wait to hear all about it. Well, I'm going to let you go. You have a good time, and don't worry about a thing. Just go ahead and enjoy your vacation."

"Thanks. I plan to do just that."

19

"Where's Lana?" I asked my parents when I returned to the dining room.

"She said for you to meet her on the beach," Mother said.

"All right. I'll see you guys around. I'm through eating," I called over my shoulder.

I went to my room and put on my swimming trunks and got a beach towel. I found Lana at a stand that rented surfboards and stuff.

"Want to try one?" I said.

"Yes." She smiled cheerfully.

Ever since we got here she had seemed mostly happy, but sometimes she became quiet and sad. I knew she was thinking about her grandfather and

Bamboo Bay. The rest of the time, though, I guess she was too interested in everything to be depressed.

"How about those?" she said, pointing to a pair.

"Cool! I've been wanting to try it."

I charged the boards to my hotel room, and we carried them to the water. They were lighter than they looked.

"So what do we do?" Lana asked.

I tried to remember movies I'd seen. "I think you lie on your stomach and paddle out till you see a wave, then stand up and ride back."

The water here was much calmer than at Bamboo Bay, but in the distance we could see big waves rolling in. We waded out till we were waist deep, then jumped on our boards and paddled side by side. The sounds of voices and traffic faded behind us, and it was just Lana and me and the ocean.

"This seems like the first time we've had together since we got out of the valley," I said.

"I know."

"Are you OK? Are you liking everything?"

"I miss the valley, but yes, I am happy. And I am glad you are here, Eric."

"Me too. Remember when we swam with the whales?"

"Yes. On the night of the full moon." She sighed. "I suppose I'll never see them again."

"Maybe they'll have some on Maui."

"Maybe." She didn't sound hopeful.

The water got rougher as we moved away from shore. I could tell by the inky color it was deep out here. I began to feel nervous as I heard waves pounding the reef.

"We don't have to surf, you know," I said. "We could just paddle around on our boards a little."

She chuckled, and I was glad to see her smile. "Don't you remember how we swam for miles?" she said.

"Yeah, but we had whales helping us."

Her smile faded. I had made her depressed again.

"Look, Lana, you've got to think about the future, not the past," I said. "There are other things in life— ouch!"

As I dipped my hands into the sea to paddle, they struck something hard.

"We're on the rocks, Lana!" I warned.

"Oh no we're not!" she shouted with a grin. Just then her surfboard rose into the air on the back of a humpback whale. A second later, mine did the same.

"They're here!" Lana yelled as the whales spouted two geysers from their blowholes behind us. The water showered down on us and we laughed.

"Do you think they're ours?" I asked.

"Of course!" Lana said.

I got to my feet on the board and pretended I was surfing. Lana did the same, and we screamed with excitement as the whales picked up speed.

Then I realized we were moving out to deep sea—fast!

"Uh, Lana," I said.

She didn't hear me.

"Lana!"

"What?"

"Aren't we, like, going the wrong way?"

She laughed. "Just wait, Eric! We've just begun!"